Yeti cool, spaghetti

CW00403610

Russell Punter

Illustrated by David Semple

High up in the mountains,
lies Yeti's Snow Café.

This hairy chef's expecting guests.

SNOW CAFÉ
BOOKINGS

TODAY:

20 members of
The Climbing Club

There's lots to do today.

He makes some fresh spaghetti,

pours water in a pot,

then lights a fire underneath
and heats it till it's hot.

Yeti adds the pasta, but...

Will this feed twenty guests?

While Yeti's food is left to cook,
he sees to things outside.

Just as he gets the tables set,
the Climbing Club arrives.

"No problem," Yeti cries.

Then... CRASH! SPLAT! SLITHER!

Here it comes...

and now it's twice the size!

Spilling from the kitchen,
and pouring through the doors,

the stream of wet spaghetti slides
and glides around their paws.

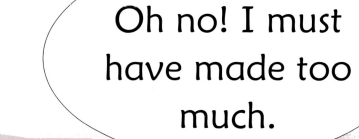

Poor Yeti just can't cope.

The pasta's going faster now.

It's flowing down the slope.

He tries a bit, but spits it out.

By now it's cold and firm.

The customers have fled in shock.

"It's all gone wrong," sighs Yeti.

Now Yeti can't cook fast enough.
His café's a success.

Starting to read

Even before children start to recognize words, they can learn about the pleasures of reading. Encouraging a love of stories and a joy in language is the best place to start.

About phonics

When children learn to read in school, they are often taught to recognize words through phonics. This teaches them to identify the sounds of letters that are then put together to make words. An important first step is for children to hear rhymes, which help them to listen out for the sounds in words.

You can find out more about phonics on the Usborne website at **usborne.com/Phonics**

Phonics Readers

These rhyming books provide the perfect combination of fun and phonics. They are lively and entertaining with great storylines and quirky illustrations. They have the added bonus of focusing on certain sounds so in this story your child will soon identify the *e* sound, as in **Yeti** and **spaghetti.** Look out, too, for rhymes such as **pot** – **hot** and **worm** – **firm.**

Reading with your child

If your child is reading a story to you, don't rush to correct mistakes, but be ready to prompt or guide if needed. Above all, give plenty of praise and encouragement.

Edited by Lesley Sims
Designed by Hope Reynolds

Reading consultants: Alison Kelly and Anne Washtell

First published in 2022 by Usborne Publishing Ltd., Usborne House, 83-85 Saffron Hill,
London EC1N 8RT, England. usborne.com Copyright © 2022 Usborne Publishing Ltd. The name
Usborne and the Balloon logo are Trade Marks of Usborne Publishing Ltd. All rights reserved.
No part of this publication may be reproduced, stored in a retrieval system or transmitted in any form
or by any means without the prior permission of the publisher. UE. First published in America in 2023.